Leo's Lavender Skirt received the International Narrating Equality Children's Book Award which celebrates its Seventh Edition.

The award was created by the Italian Association *Woman to be* in order to promote equality and diversity and challenge stereotypes in literature.

To Nico, with you I learn every day.

Irma Borges

Leo's Lavender Skirt

Egalité Series

© Text: Irma Borges, 2022
© Illustrations: Francesco Fagnani, 2022
© Edition: NubeOcho, 2022
© Translation: Cecilia Ross, 2022
www.nubeocho.com · hello@nubeocho.com

Original title: *La falda morada de Leo*

Text Editing: Caroline Dookie, Rebecca Packard

First edition: October, 2022
ISBN: 978-84-18599-74-3
Legal Deposit: M-3443-2022

Printed in Portugal.

 Fondazione Cassa di Risparmio di Lucca
 FONDAZIONE BANCA DEL MONTE DI LUCCA
 Città di Lucca
 PROVINCIA di Lucca
 COMUNE DI CAPANNORI
 pari opportunità

 USCIRE DAL GUSCIO: EDUCARE ALLE DIFFERENZE. FESTIVAL DI LETTERATURA PER L'INFANZIA E L'ADOLESCENZA QUINTA EDIZIONE
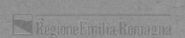 Regione Emilia-Romagna
 CITTÀ METROPOLITANA DI BOLOGNA
 UNIONE RENO GALLIERA
 Associazione Genitori Rilassati San Pietro in Casale

LEO's
LAVENDER SKIRT

Irma Borges
Francesco Fagnani

nubeOCHO

Leo has a treasure chest where he keeps
all his precious costumes.

He likes to dress up as a pirate, a superhero,
and even a knight in shining armor!

Among his many costumes, there's a lavender skirt that Leo holds very dear. He wears it to dress up as many, many characters.

Sometimes, Leo goes out wearing his costumes. And one day, he put on his lavender skirt.

Leo sat behind his mom on the bicycle,
and as he often did, he began singing.

When they stopped at a traffic light,
a lady smiled and said:

"What a pretty girl, and so cheerful!
Do you like singing?"

Leo's smile turned into a frown. The lady didn't notice, because at that moment the traffic light went green, but Leo asked his mom:

"Why did she say I was a girl? I am a boy!"

"Of course you are," his
mother replied. "Don't let it
bother you."

But it did bother Leo.
When they got back home, he shouted:

"I will never wear my lavender skirt again!"

His dad, who was making dinner, asked:

"What happened?"

"A lady called me a girl, and I'm a boy!"

Dad sat by Leo's side and looked deep into his eyes. He explained to him that there once existed, and still exist today, places where everyone, including men and boys, wear dresses and skirts.

Dad said he'd love to have one—they looked quite comfortable, especially in summer. Leo imagined him and his father traveling to those places.

The next day, before school, Leo rummaged
inside his treasure chest and found some leggings.
He put them on along with his lavender skirt on top.

"Leo, do you really want to go to school dressed like this?" his mother asked.

"I do!" Leo replied, more determined than ever.

His mom looked at him for a moment, and Leo completely understood what she meant with that look.

"I like my lavender skirt and I'm not going to stop wearing it. If they say I'm a girl, I'll tell them I'm a boy!" he said calmly.

"Mom, did you know that there are places
in the world where men wear skirts?"

"I do. And did you know that long ago
women were not allowed to wear trousers?"

Leo's mom told him that, many years ago, a girl named Fanny wore trousers, even though all other girls wore dresses and skirts.

After Fanny, there were many others: Mary, Luisa, Marlene… Some of them were even banned from going out in public in trousers.

Fanny Wright

Leo thought about all those women that had defied
the rules. Maybe he could dress as he wanted to as well.

Leo smiled, and taking his mom's hand,
he walked out of the house in his lavender skirt.